TWO STORIES
BY ONE OF THE GREATS
OF OCCULT WRITING

BY

MADAME HELENA BLAVATSKY

British Library Cataloguing-in-Publication Data
A catalogue record for this book is available from the
British Library

CONTENTS

HELENA BLAVATSKY

Helena Petrovna Blavatsky was born in Yekaterinoslav, the Russian Empire (modern-day Ukraine) in 1831. Writing was in her family; her mother, who wrote under the pseudonym George Sand, was a world-famous author, and her sister was a prolific writer of occult and fantastic fiction. Blavatsky fled her unhappy first marriage when she was just eighteen, and began a life of travel by abandoning her family and sailing to Istanbul.

Between 1848 and 1858, she travelled far and wide, exploring almost every continent and spending several extended spells in Tibet. By this time, Blavatsky had established herself as a medium and begun to hold séances, and when she emigrated to New York City in 1873, people were impressed with her professed psychic abilities. At a time when mediumship was a burgeoning (and not so sceptically viewed) psychical science, she became a popular figure. Throughout her career she claimed to have demonstrated feats including levitation, clairvoyance, telepathy and telekinesis.

In 1875, she founded The Theosophical Society, and in 1877, she published her *Isis Unveiled*–her first major work on theosophy, examining religion and science in the light of Western and Oriental ancient wisdom and occult and spiritualistic phenomena. The book was a major success, further cementing her fame. In 1879, she moved to Bombay, India, where she converted to Buddhism and continued to expand the Society. In 1888, she published her *magnum opus, The Secret Doctrine.*

Suffering from Bright's disease and complications from influenza, Blavatsky died in her London home in 1891. Her last words were "Keep the link unbroken! Do not let my last incarnation be a failure." After her death, she has developed a polarising reputation; her supporters see her as a visionary and a spiritual genius, her detractors as a charlatan and a fraud.

THE ENSOULED VIOLIN

Helena Blavatsky

1

In the year 1828, an old German, a music teacher, came to Paris with his pupil and settled unostentatiously in one of the quiet *faubourgs* of the metropolis. The first rejoiced in the name of Samuel Klaus; the second answered to the more poetical appellation of Franz Stenio. The younger man was a violinist, gifted, as rumour went, with extraordinary, almost miraculous talent. Yet as he was poor and had not hitherto made a name for himself in Europe, he remained for several years in the capital of France–the heart and pulse of capricious continental fashion–unknown and unappreciated. Franz was a Styrian by birth, and, at the time of the event to be presently described, he was a young man considerably under thirty. A philosopher and a dreamer by nature, imbued with all the mystic oddities of true genius, he reminded one of some of the heroes in Hoffmann's *Contes Fantastiques*. His earlier existence had been a very unusual, in fact, quite an eccentric one, and its history must be briefly told—for the better understanding of the present story.

Born of very pious country people, in a quiet burg among the Styrian Alps; nursed 'by the native gnomes who watched over his cradle'; growing up in the weird atmosphere of the ghouls and vampires who play such a prominent part in the household of every Styrian and Slavonian in Southern Austria; educated later, as a student, in the shadow of the old Rhenish castles of Germany; Franz from his childhood had passed through every emotional stage on the plane of the so-called 'supernatural'. He had also studied at one time the 'occult arts' with an enthusiastic disciple of Paracelsus and Kunrath; alchemy had few theoretical secrets for him; and he had dabbled in 'ceremonial magic' and 'sorcery' with some Hungarian Tziganes. Yet he loved above all else music, and above music—his violin.

At the age of twenty-two he suddenly gave up his practical studies in the occult, and from that day, though as devoted as ever in thought to the beautiful Grecian Gods, he surrendered himself entirely to his art. Of his classic studies he had retained only that which related to the muses—Euterpe especially, at whose altar he worshipped—and Orpheus whose magic lyre he tried to emulate with his violin. Except his dreamy belief in the nymphs and the sirens, on account probably of the double relationship of the latter to the muses through Calliope and Orpheus, he was interested but little in the matters of this sublunary world. All his aspirations mounted, like incense, with the wave of the heavenly harmony that he drew from his instrument, to a higher and a nobler sphere. He dreamed awake, and lived a real though an enchanted life only during those hours when his magic bow carried him along the wave of sound to the Pagan Olympus, to the feet of Euterpe. A strange child he had ever been in his own home, where tales of magic and witchcraft grow out of every inch of the soil; a still stranger boy he had become, until finally he had blossomed into manhood, without one single characteristic of youth. Never had a fair face attracted his attention; not for one moment had his thoughts turned from his solitary studies to a life beyond that of a mystic Bohemian. Content with his own company, he had thus passed the best years of his youth and manhood with his violin for his chief idol, and with the Gods and Goddesses of old Greece for his audience, in perfect ignorance of practical life. His whole existence had been one long day of dreams, of melody and sunlight, and he had never felt any other aspirations.

How useless, but oh, how glorious those dreams! how vivid! and why should he desire any better fate? Was he not all that he wanted to be, transformed in a second of thought into one or another hero; from Orpheus, who held all nature breathless, to the urchin who piped away under the plane tree to the naiads of Calirrhoë's crystal fountain? Did not the swift-footed nymphs frolic at his beck and call to the sound of the magic

flute of the Arcadian shepherd–who was himself? Behold, the
Goddess of Love and Beauty herself descending from on high,
attracted by the sweet-voiced notes of his violin! . . . Yet there
came a time when he preferred Syrinx to Aphrodite–not as the
fair nymph pursued by Pan, but after her transformation by
the merciful Gods into the reed out of which the frustrated
God of the Shepherds had made his magic pipe. For also, with
time, ambition grows and is rarely satisfied. When he tried to
emulate on his violin the enchanting sounds that resounded in his mind, the whole of Parnassus kept silent under the
spell, or joined in heavenly chorus; but the audience he finally
craved was composed of more than the Gods sung by Hesiod,
verily of the most appreciative *mélomanes* of European capi-
tals. He felt jealous of the magic pipe, and would fain have
had it at his command.

'Oh! that I could allure a nymph into my beloved violin!'–
he often cried, after awakening from one of his daydreams.
'Oh, that I could only span in spirit flight the abyss of Time!
Oh, that I could find myself for one short day a partaker of the
secret arts of the Gods, a God myself, in the sight and hearing of enraptured humanity; and, having learned the mystery
of the lyre of Orpheus, or secured within my violin a siren,
thereby benefit mortals to my own glory!'

Thus, having for long years dreamed in the company of the
Gods of his fancy, he now took to dreaming of the transitory
glories of fame upon this earth. But at this time he was sud-

denly called home by his widowed mother from one of the German universities where he had lived for the last year or two. This was an event which brought his plans to an end, at least so far as the immediate future was concerned, for he had hitherto drawn upon her alone for his meagre pittance, and his means were not sufficient for an independent life outside his native place.

His return had a very unexpected result. His mother, whose only love he was on earth, died soon after she had welcomed her Benjamin back; and the good wives of the burg exercised their swift tongues for many a month after as to the real causes of that death.

Frau Stenio, before Franz's return, was a healthy, buxom, middle-aged body, strong and hearty. She was a pious and a God-fearing soul too, who had never failed in saying her prayers, nor had missed an early mass for years during his absence. On the first Sunday after her son had settled at home—a day that she had been longing for and had anticipated for months in joyous visions, in which she saw him kneeling by her side in the little church on the hill—she called him from the foot of the stairs. The hour had come when her pious dream was to be realized, and she was waiting for him, carefully wiping the dust from the prayer-book he had used in his boyhood. But instead of Franz, it was his violin that responded to her call, mixing its sonorous voice with the other cracked tones of the peal of the merry Sunday bells. The fond mother was somewhat shocked at hearing the prayer-inspiring sounds drowned by the weird, fantastic notes of the 'Dance of the Witches'; they seemed to her so unearthly and mocking. But she almost fainted upon hearing the definite refusal of her well-beloved son to go to church. He never went to church, he coolly remarked. It was a loss of time; besides which, the loud peals of the old church organ jarred on his nerves. Nothing should induce him to submit to the torture of listening to that cracked organ. He was firm, and nothing could move him. To her supplications and remonstrances he put an end by offering to play for her a 'Hymn to the Sun' he had just composed.

From that memorable Sunday morning, Frau Stenio lost her usual serenity of mind. She hastened to lay her sorrows and seek for consolation at the foot of the confessional; but that which she heard in response from the stern priest filled her gentle and unsophisticated soul with dismay and almost with despair. A feeling of fear, a sense of profound terror, which soon became a chronic state with her, pursued her from that moment; her nights became disturbed and sleepless, her days passed in prayer and lamentations. In her maternal anxiety for the salvation of her beloved son's soul, and for his *post mortem* welfare, she made a series of rash vows. Finding that neither the Latin petition to the Mother of God written for her by her spiritual adviser, nor yet the humble supplications in German, addressed by herself to every saint she had reason to believe was residing in Paradise, worked the desired effect, she took to pilgrimages to distant shrines. During one of these journeys to a holy chapel situated high up in the mountains, she caught cold, amidst the glaciers of the Tyrol, and redescended only to take to a sick bed, from which she arose no more. Frau Stenio's vow had led her, in one sense, to the desired result. The poor woman was now given an opportunity of seeking out in *propria persona* the saints she had believed in so well, and of pleading face to face for the recreant son, who refused adherence to them and to the Church, scoffed at monk and confessional, and held the organ in such horror.

Franz sincerely lamented his mother's death. Unaware of being the indirect cause of it, he felt no remorse; but selling the modest household goods and chattels, light in purse and heart, he resolved to travel on foot for a year or two, before settling down to any definite profession.

A hazy desire to see the great cities of Europe, and to try his luck in France, lurked at the bottom of this travelling project, but his Bohemian habits of life were too strong to be abruptly abandoned. He placed his small capital with a banker for a rainy day, and started on his pedestrian journey via Germany and Austria. His violin paid for his board and lodging in the inns and farms on his way, and he passed his days in the green fields and in the solemn silent woods, face to face with Nature, dreaming all the time as usual with his eyes open. During the three months of his pleasant travels to and fro, he never descended for one moment from Parnassus; but, as an alchemist transmutes lead into gold, so he transformed everything on his way into a song of Hesiod or Anacreon. Every evening, while fiddling for his supper and bed, whether on a green lawn or in the hall of a rustic inn, his fancy changed the whole scene for him. Village swains and maidens became transfigured into Arcadian shepherds and nymphs. The sand-covered floor was now a green sward; the uncouth couples spinning round in a measured waltz with the wild grace of tamed bears became priests and priestesses of Terpsichore; the bulky, cherry-cheeked and blue-eyed daughters of rural Germany were the Hesperides circling around the trees laden with the golden apples. Nor did the melodious strains of the Arcadian demigods piping on their syrinxes, and audible but to his own enchanted ear, vanish with the dawn. For no sooner was the curtain of sleep raised from his eyes than he would sally forth into a new magic realm of daydreams. On his way to some dark and solemn pine-forest, he played incessantly, to himself and to everything else. He fiddled to the green hill, and forthwith the mountain and the moss-covered rocks moved forward to hear him the better, as they had done at the sound of the Orphean lyre. He fiddled to the merry-voiced brook, to the hurrying river, and both slackened their speed and stopped their waves, and, becoming silent, seemed to listen to him in an entranced rapture. Even the long-legged stork who stood meditatively on one leg on the thatched top of the rustic mill, gravely resolving unto himself the problem of his too-long existence, sent out after him a long and strident cry, screeching, 'art thou Orpheus himself, O Stenio?'

It was a period of full bliss, of a daily and almost hourly exaltation. The last words of his dying mother, whispering to him of the horrors of eternal condemnation, had left him unaffected, and the only vision her warning evoked in him was that of Pluto. By a ready association of ideas, he saw the lord of the dark nether kingdom greeting him as he had greeted the husband of Eurydice before him. Charmed with the magic sounds of his violin, the wheel of Ixion was at a standstill once more, thus affording relief to the wretched seducer of Juno, and giving the lie to those who claim eternity for the duration of the punishment of condemned sinners. He perceived Tantalus forgetting his never-ceasing thirst, and smacking his lips as he drank in the heaven-born melody; the stone of Sisyphus becoming motionless, the Furies themselves smiling on him, and the sovereign of the gloomy regions delighted, and awarding preference to his violin over the lyre of Orpheus. Taken *au sérieux*, mythology thus seems a decided antidote to fear, in the face of theological threats, especially when strengthened with an insane and passionate love of music; with Franz, Euterpe proved always victorious in every contest, aye, even with Hell itself!

But there is an end to everything, and very soon Franz had to give up uninterrupted dreaming. He had reached the university town where dwelt his old violin teacher, Samuel Klaus. When this antiquated musician found that his beloved and favourite pupil, Franz, had been left poor in purse and still poorer in earthly affections, he felt his strong attachment to the boy awaken with tenfold force. He took Franz to his heart, and forthwith adopted him as his son.

The old teacher reminded people of one of those grotesque figures which look as if they had just stepped out of some medieval panel. And yet Klaus, with his fantastic *allures* of a night-goblin, had the most loving heart, as tender as that of a woman, and the self-sacrificing nature of an old Christian martyr. When Franz had briefly narrated to him the history of his last few years, the professor took him by the hand, and leading him into his study simply said:

'Stop with me, and put an end to your Bohemian life. Make yourself famous. I am old and childless and will be your father. Let us live together and forget all save fame.'

And forthwith he offered to proceed with Franz to Paris, *via* several large German cities, where they would stop to give concerts.

In a few days Klaus succeeded in making Franz forget his vagrant life and its artistic independence, and reawakened in his pupil his now dormant ambition and desire for worldly fame. Hitherto, since his mother's death, he had been content to receive applause only from the Gods and Goddesses who inhabited his vivid fancy; now he began to crave once more for the admiration of mortals. Under the clever and careful training of old Klaus his remarkable talent gained in strength and powerful charm with every day, and his reputation grew and expanded with every city and town wherein he made himself heard. His ambition was being rapidly realized; the presiding genii of various musical centres to whose patronage his talent was submitted soon proclaimed him *the one* violinist of the day, and the public declared loudly that he stood unrivalled by any one whom they had ever heard. These laudations very soon made both master and pupil completely lose their heads.

But Paris was less ready with such appreciation. Paris makes reputations for itself, and will take none on faith. They had been living in it for almost three years, and were still climbing with difficulty the artist's Calvary, when an event occurred which put an end even to their most modest expectations. The first arrival of Niccolo Paganini was suddenly heralded, and threw Lutetia into a convulsion of expectation. The unparalleled artist arrived, and–all Paris fell at once at his feet.

2

Now it is a well-known fact that a superstition born in the dark days of medieval superstition, and surviving almost to the middle of the present century, attributed all such abnormal, out-of-the-way talent as that of Paganini to 'supernatural' agency. Every great and marvellous artist had been accused in his day of dealings with the devil. A few instances will suffice to refresh the reader's memory.

Tartini, the great composer and violinist of the XVIIth century, was denounced as one who got his best inspirations from the Evil One, with whom he was, it was said, in regular league. This accusation was, of course, due to the almost magical impression he produced upon his audiences. His inspired performance on the violin secured for him in his native country the title of 'Master of Nations'. The *Sonate du Diable*, also called 'Tartini's Dream'—as everyone who has heard it will be ready to testify—is the most weird melody ever heard or invented: hence, the marvellous composition has become the source of endless legends. Nor were they entirely baseless, since it was he, himself, who was shown to have originated them. Tartini confessed to having written it on awakening from a dream, in which he had heard his sonata performed by Satan, for his benefit, and in consequence of a bargain made with his infernal majesty.

Several famous singers, even, whose exceptional voices

struck the hearers with superstitious admiration, have not escaped a like accusation. Pasta's splendid voice was attributed in her day to the fact that, three months before her birth, the diva's mother was carried during a trance to heaven, and there treated to a vocal concert of seraphs. Malibran was indebted for her voice to St Cecelia, while others said she owed it to a demon who watched over her cradle and sung the baby to sleep. Finally, Paganini–the unrivalled performer, the mean Italian, who like Dryden's Jubal striking on the 'chorded shell' forced the throngs that followed him to worship the divine sounds produced, and made people say that 'less than a God could not dwell within the hollow of his violin'–Paganini left a legend too.

The almost supernatural art of the greatest violin-player that the world has ever known was often speculated upon, never understood. The effect produced by him on his audience was literally marvellous, overpowering. The great Rossini is said to have wept like a sentimental German maiden on hearing him play for the first time. The Princess Elisa of Lucca, a sister of the great Napoleon, in whose service Paganini was, as director of her private orchestra, for a long time was unable to hear him play without fainting. In women he produced nervous fits and hysterics at his will; stout-hearted men he drove to frenzy. He changed cowards into heroes and made the bravest soldiers feel like so many nervous schoolgirls. Is it to be wondered at, then, that hundreds of weird tales circulated for long years about and around the mysterious Genoese, that modern Orpheus of Europe. One of these was especially ghastly. It was rumoured, and was believed by more people than would probably like to confess it, that the strings of his violin Were made of *human intestines, according to all the rules and requirements of the Black Art.*

Exaggerated as this idea may seem to some, it has nothing impossible in it; and it is more than probable that it was this legend that led to the extraordinary events which we are about to narrate. Human organs are often used by the Eastern Black Magician, so-called, and it is an averred fact that some Bengâlî Tântrikas (reciters of *tantras*, or 'invocations to the demon', as a reverend writer has described them) use human corpses, and certain internal and external organs pertaining to them, as powerful magical agents for bad purposes.

However this may be, now that the magnetic and mesmeric potencies of hypnotism are recognized as facts by most physicians, it may be suggested with less danger than heretofore that the extraordinary effects of Paganini's violin-playing were not, perhaps, entirely due to his talent and genius. The wonder and awe he so easily excited were as much caused by his external appearance, 'which had something weird and demoniacal in it', according to certain of his biographers, as by the inexpressible charm of his execution and his remarkable mechanical skill. The latter is demonstrated by his perfect imitation of the flageolet, and his performance of long and magnificent melodies on the G string alone. In this performance, which many an artist has tried to copy without success, he remains unrivalled to this day.

It is owing to this remarkable appearance of his–termed by his friends eccentric, and by his too nervous victims, diabolical–that he experienced great difficulties in refuting certain ugly rumours. These were credited far more easily in his day than they would be now. It was whispered throughout Italy, and even in his own native town, that Paganini had murdered his wife, and, later on, a mistress, both of whom he had loved passionately, and both of whom he had not hesitated to sacrifice to his fiendish ambition. He had made himself proficient in magic arts, it was asserted, and had succeeded thereby in imprisoning the souls of his two victims in his violin–his famous Cremona.

It is maintained by the immediate friends of Ernst T. W. Hoffmann, the celebrated author of *Die Elixire des Teufels, Meister Martin*, and other charming and mystical tales, that Councillor Crespel, in the *Violin of Cremona*, was taken from the legend about Paganini. It is, as all who have read it know, the history of a celebrated violin, into which the voice and the soul of a famous diva, a woman whom Crespel had loved and killed, had passed, and to which was added the voice of his beloved daughter, Antonia.

Nor was this superstition utterly ungrounded, nor was Hoffmann to be blamed for adopting it, after he had heard

Paganini's playing. The extraordinary facility with which the artist drew out of his instrument, not only the most unearthly sounds, but positively human voices, justified the suspicion. Such effects might well have startled an audience and thrown terror into many a nervous heart. Add to this the impenetrable mystery connected with a certain period of Paganini's youth, and the most wild tales about him must be found in a measure justifiable, and even excusable; especially among a nation whose ancestors knew the Borgias and the Medicis of Black Art fame.

3

In those pre-telegraphic days, newspapers were limited, and the wings of fame had a heavier flight than they have now.

Franz had hardly heard of Paganini; and when he did, he swore he would rival, if not eclipse, the Genoese magician. Yes, he would either become the most famous of all living violinists, or he would break his instrument and put an end to his life at the same time.

Old Klaus rejoiced at such a determination. He rubbed his hands in glee, and jumping about on his lame leg like a crippled satyr, he flattered and incensed his pupil, believing himself all the while to be performing a sacred duty to the holy and majestic cause of art.

Upon first setting foot in Paris, three years before, Franz had all but failed. Musical critics pronounced him a rising star, but had all agreed that he required a few more years' practice, before he could hope to carry his audiences by storm. Therefore, after a desperate study of over two years and uninterrupted preparations, the Styrian artist had finally made himself ready for his first serious appearance in the great Opera House where a public concert before the most exacting critics of the old world was to be held; at this critical moment Paganini's arrival in the European metropolis placed an obstacle in the way of the realization of his hopes, and the old German professor wisely postponed his pupil's *début*. At first he had simply smiled at the wild enthusiasm, the laudatory hymns sung about the Genoese violinist, and the almost superstitious awe with which his name was pronounced. But very soon Paganini's name became a burning iron in the hearts of both the artists, and a threatening phantom in the mind of Klaus. A few days more, and they shuddered at the very mention of their great rival, whose success became with every night more unprecedented.

The first series of concerts was over, but neither Klaus nor Franz had as yet had an opportunity of hearing him and of judging for themselves. So great and so beyond their means was the charge for admission, and so small the hope of getting a free pass from a brother artist justly regarded as the meanest of men in monetary transactions, that they had to wait for a chance, as did so many others. But the day came when neither master nor pupil could control their impatience any longer; so they pawned their watches, and with the proceeds bought two modest seats.

Who can describe the enthusiasm, the triumphs, of this famous, and at the same time fatal night! The audience was frantic; men wept and women screamed and fainted, while both Klaus and Stenio sat looking paler than two ghosts. At the first touch of Paganini's magic bow, both Franz and Samuel felt as if the icy hand of death had touched them. Carried away by an irresistible enthusiasm, which turned into a violent, unearthly mental torture, they dared neither look into each other's faces, nor exchange one word during the whole performance.

At midnight, while the chosen delegates of the Musical Societies and the Conservatory of Paris unhitched the horses, and dragged the carriage of the grand artist home in triumph, the two Germans returned to their modest lodging, and it was a pitiful sight to see them. Mournful and desperate, they placed themselves in their usual seats at the fire-corner, and neither for a while opened his mouth.

'Samuel!' at last exclaimed Franz, pale as death itself. 'Samuel–it remains for us now but to die! . . . Do you hear me? . . . We are worthless! We were two madmen to have ever hoped that anyone in this world would ever rival . . . him!'

The name of Paganini stuck in his throat, as in utter despair he fell into his armchair.

The old professor's wrinkles suddenly became purple. His little greenish eyes gleamed phosphorescently as, bending towards his pupil, he whispered to him in hoarse and broken tones:

'*Nein, nein!* Thou art wrong, my Franz! I have taught thee, and thou hast learned all of the great art that a simple mortal, and a Christian by baptism, can learn from another simple mortal. Am I to blame because these accursed Italians, in order to reign unequalled in the domain of art, have recourse to Satan and the diabolical effects of Black Magic?'

Franz turned his eyes upon his old master. There was a sinister light burning in those glittering orbs; a light telling plainly, that, to secure such a power, he, too, would not scruple to sell himself, body and soul, to the Evil One.

But he said not a word, and, turning his eyes from his old master's face, gazed dreamily at the dying embers.

The same long-forgotten incoherent dreams, which, after seeming such realities to him in his younger days, had been given up entirely, and had gradually faded from his mind, now crowded back into it with the same force and vividness as of old. The grimacing shades of Ixion, Sisyphus and Tantalus resurrected and stood before him, saying:

'What matters hell–in which thou believest not. And even if hell there be, it is the hell described by the old Greeks, not that of the modern bigots–a locality full of conscious shadows, to whom thou canst be a second Orpheus.'

Franz felt that he was going mad, and, turning instinctively, he looked his old master once more right in the face. Then his bloodshot eye evaded the gaze of Klaus.

Whether Samuel understood the terrible state of mind of his pupil, or whether he wanted to draw him out, to make him speak, and thus to divert his thoughts, must remain as hypothetical to the reader as it is to the writer. Whatever may have been in his mind, the German enthusiast went on, speaking with a feigned calmness:

'Franz, my dear boy, I tell you that the art of the accursed Italian is not natural; that it is due neither to study nor to genius. It never was acquired in the usual, natural way. You need not stare at me in that wild manner, for what I say is in the mouth of millions of people. Listen to what I now tell you, and try to understand. You have heard the strange tale whispered about the famous Tartini? He died one fine Sabbath night, strangled by his familiar demon, who had taught him how to endow his violin with a human voice, by shutting up in it, by means of incantations, the soul of a young virgin. Paganini did more. In order to endow his instrument with the faculty of emitting human sounds, such as sobs, despairing cries, supplications, moans of love and fury–in short, the most heartrending notes of the human voice–Paganini became the murderer not only of his wife and his mistress, but also of a friend, who was more tenderly attached to him than any other being on this earth. He then made the four chords of his magic violin out of the intestines of his last victim. This is the secret of his enchanting talent, of that overpowering melody, that combination of sounds, which you will never be able to master unless . . .'

The old man could not finish the sentence. He staggered back before the fiendish look of his pupil, and covered his face with his hands.

Franz was breathing heavily, and his eyes had an expression which reminded Klaus of those of a hyena. His pallor was cadaverous. For some time he could not speak, but only gasped for breath. At last he slowly muttered:

'Are you in earnest?'

'I am, as I hope to help you.'

'And . . . and do you really believe that had I only the means of obtaining human intestines for strings, I could rival Paganini?' asked Franz, after a moment's pause, and casting down his eyes.

The old German unveiled his face, and, with a strange look of determination upon it, softly answered:

'Human intestines alone are not sufficient for our purpose; they must have belonged to someone who had loved us well, with an unselfish, holy love. Tartini endowed his violin with the life of a virgin; but that virgin had died of unrequited love for him. The fiendish artist had prepared beforehand a tube, in which he managed to catch her last breath as she expired, pronouncing his beloved name, and he then transferred this breath to his violin. As to Paganini, I have just told you his tale. It was with the consent of his victim, though, that he murdered him to get possession of his intestines.

'Oh, for the power of the human voice!' Samuel went on, after a brief pause. 'What can equal the eloquence, the magic spell of the human voice? Do you think, my poor boy, I would not have taught you this great, this final secret, were it not that it throws one right into the clutches of him . . . who must remain unnamed at night?' he added, with a sudden return to the superstitions of his youth.

Franz did not answer; but with a calmness awful to behold,

24

he left his place, took down the violin from the wall where it was hanging, and, with one powerful grasp of the chords, he tore them out and flung them into the fire.

Samuel suppressed a cry of horror. The chords were hissing upon the coals, where, among the blazing logs, they wriggled and curled like so many living snakes.

'By the witches of Thessaly and the dark arts of Circe!' he exclaimed, with foaming mouth and his eyes burning like coals; 'by the Furies of Hell and Pluto himself, I now swear, in thy presence, O Samuel, my master, never to touch a violin again until I can string it with four human chords. May I be accursed for ever and ever if I do!' He fell senseless on the floor, with a deep sob, that ended like a funeral wail; old Samuel lifted him up as he would have lifted a child, and carried him to his bed. Then he sallied forth in search of a physician.

4

For several days after this painful scene Franz was very ill, ill almost beyond recovery. The physician declared him to be suffering from brain fever and said that the worst was to be feared. For nine long days the patient remained delirious; and Klaus, who was nursing him night and day with the solicitude of the tenderest mother, was horrified at the work of his own hands. For the first time since their acquaintance began, the old teacher, owing to the wild ravings of his pupil, was able to penetrate into the darkest corners of that weird, superstitious, cold, and, at the same time, passionate nature; and–he trembled at what he discovered. For he saw that which he had failed to perceive before–Franz as he was in reality, and not as he seemed to superficial observers. Music was the life of the young man, and adulation was the air he breathed, without which that life became a burden; from the chords of his violin alone, Stenio drew his life and being, but the applause of men and even of Gods was necessary to its support. He saw unveiled before his eyes a genuine, artistic, *earthly* soul, with its divine counterpart totally absent, a son of the Muses, all fancy and brain poetry, but without a heart. While listening to the ravings of that delirious and unhinged fancy Klaus felt as if he were for the first time in his long life exploring a marvellous and untravelled region, a human nature not of this world but of some incomplete planet. He saw all this, and shuddered.

More than once he asked himself whether it would not be doing a kindness to his 'boy' to let him die before he returned to consciousness.

But he loved his pupil too well to dwell for long on such an idea. Franz had bewitched his truly artistic nature, and now old Klaus felt as though their two lives were inseparably linked together. That he could thus feel was a revelation to the old man; so he decided to save Franz, even at the expense of his own old and, as he thought, useless life.

The seventh day of the illness brought on a most terrible crisis. For twenty-four hours the patient never closed his eyes, nor remained for a moment silent; he raved continuously during the whole time. His visions were peculiar, and he minutely described each. Fantastic, ghastly figures kept slowly swimming out of the penumbra of his small, dark room, in regular and uninterrupted procession, and he greeted each by name as he might greet old acquaintances. He referred to himself as Prometheus, bound to the rock by four bands made of human intestines. At the foot of the Caucasian Mount the black waters of the river Styx were running . . . They had deserted Arcadia, and were now endeavouring to encircle within a seven-fold embrace the rock upon which he was suffering . . .

'Wouldst thou know the name of the Promethean rock, old man?' he roared into his adopted father's ear . . .'Listen then . . . its name is . . . called . . . Samuel Klaus . . .'

'Yes, yes! . . .' the German murmured disconsolately. 'It

is I who killed him, while seeking to console. The news of Paganini's magic arts struck his fancy too vividly . . . Oh, my poor, poor boy!'

'Ha, ha, ha, ha!' The patient broke into a loud and discordant laugh. 'Aye, poor old man, sayest thou? . . . So, so, thou art of poor stuff, anyhow, and wouldst look well only when stretched upon a fine Cremona violin! . . .'

Klaus shuddered, but said nothing. He only bent over the poor maniac, and with a kiss upon his brow, a caress as tender and as gentle as that of a doting mother, he left the sick-room for a few instants, to seek relief in his own garret. When he returned, the ravings were following another channel. Franz was singing, trying to imitate the sounds of a violin.

Towards the evening of that day, the delirium of the sick man became perfectly ghastly. He saw spirits of fire clutching at his violin. Their skeleton hands, from each finger of which grew a flaming claw, beckoned to old Samuel . . . They approached and surrounded the old master, and were preparing to rim him open . . . him, 'the only man on this earth who loves me with an unselfish, holy love, and . . . whose intestines can be of any good at all!' he went on whispering, with glaring eyes and demon laugh . . .

By the next morning, however, the fever had disappeared, and by the end of the ninth day Stenio had left his bed, having no recollection of his illness, and no suspicion that he had allowed Klaus to read his inner thought. Nay; had he himself any knowledge that such a horrible idea as the sacrifice of his old master to his ambition had ever entered his mind? Hardly. The only immediate result of his fatal illness was, that as, by reason of his vow, his artistic passion could find no issue, another passion awoke, which might avail to feed his ambition and his insatiable fancy. He plunged headlong into the study of the Occult Arts, of Alchemy and of Magic. In the practice of Magic the young dreamer sought to stifle the voice of his passionate longing for his, as he thought, for ever lost violin . . .

Weeks and months passed away, and the conversation about Paganini was never resumed between the master and the pupil. But a profound melancholy had taken possession of Franz, the two hardly exchanged a word, the violin hung mute, chordless, full of dust, in its habitual place. It was as the presence of a soulless corpse between them.

The young man had become gloomy and sarcastic, even avoiding the mention of music. Once, as his old professor, after long hesitation, took out his own violin from its dust-covered case and prepared to play, Franz gave a convulsive shudder, but said nothing. At the first notes of the bow, however, he glared like a madman, and rushing out of the house, remained for hours, wandering in the streets. Then old Samuel in his turn threw his instrument down, and locked himself up in his room till the following morning.

One night as Franz sat, looking particularly pale and

gloomy, old Samuel suddenly jumped from his seat, and after hopping about the room in a magpie fashion, approached his pupil, imprinted a fond kiss upon the young man's brow, and squeaked at the top of his shrill voice:

'Is it not time to put an end to all this? . . .'

Whereupon, starting from his usual lethargy, Franz echoed, as in a dream:

'Yes, it is time to put an end to this.'

Upon which the two separated, and went to bed.

On the following morning, when Franz awoke, he was astonished not to see his old teacher in his usual place to greet him. But he had greatly altered during the last few months, and he at first paid no attention to his absence, unusual as it was. He dressed and went into the adjoining room, a little parlour where they had their meals, and which separated their two bedrooms. The fire had not been lighted since the embers had died out on the previous night, and no sign was anywhere visible of the professor's busy hand in his usual housekeeping duties. Greatly puzzled, but in no way dismayed, Franz took his usual place at the corner of the now cold fireplace, and fell into an aimless reverie. As he stretched himself in his old arm-chair, raising both his hands to clasp them behind his head in a favourite posture of his, his hand came into contact with something on a shelf at his back; he knocked against a case, and brought it violently to the ground.

It was old Klaus's violin-case that came down to the floor

with such a sudden crash that the case opened and the violin fell out of it, rolling to the feet of Franz. And then the chords, striking against the brass fender emitted a sound, prolonged, sad and mournful as the sigh of an unrestful soul; it seemed to fill the whole room, and reverberated in the head and the very heart of the young man. The effect of that broken violin-string was magical.

'Samuel!' cried Stenio, with his eyes starting from their sockets, and an unknown terror suddenly taking possession of his whole being. 'Samuel! what has happened? . . . My good, my dear old master!' he called out, hastening to the professor's little room, and throwing the door violently open. No one answered, all was silent within.

He staggered back, frightened at the sound of his own voice, so changed and hoarse it seemed to him at this moment. No reply came in response to his call. Naught followed but a dead silence . . . that stillness which, in the domain of sounds, usually denotes death. In the presence of a corpse, as in the lugubrious stillness of a tomb, such silence acquires a mysterious power, which strikes the sensitive soul with a nameless terror . . . The little room was dark, and Franz hastened to open the shutters.

Samuel was lying on his bed, cold, stiff, and lifeless . . . At the sight of the corpse of him who had loved him so well, and had been to him more than a father, Franz experienced a dreadful revulsion of feeling, a terrible shock. But the ambition of the fanatical artist got the better of the despair of the man, and smothered the feelings of the latter in a few seconds.

A note bearing his own name was conspicuously placed upon a table near the corpse. With trembling hand, the violinist tore open the envelope, and read the following:

My beloved son, Franz,

When you read this, I shall have made the greatest sacrifice, that your best and only friend and teacher could have accomplished for your fame. He, who loved you most, is now but an inanimate lump of clay. Of your old teacher there now remains but a clod of cold organic matter. I need not prompt you as to what you have to do with it. Fear not stupid prejudices. It is for your future fame that I have made an offering of my body, and you would be guilty of the blackest ingratitude were you now to render useless this sacrifice. When you shall have replaced the chords upon your violin, and these chords a portion of my own self, under your touch it will acquire the power of that accursed sorcerer, all the magic voices of Paganini's instrument. You will find therein my voice, my sighs and groans, my song of welcome, the prayerful sobs of my infinite and sorrowful sympathy, my love for you. And now, my Franz, fear nobody! Take your instrument with you, and dog the steps of him who filled our lives with bitterness and despair! . . . Appear in every arena, where, hitherto, he has reigned without a rival, and bravely throw the gauntlet of defiance in his face. O Franz! then only wilt thou hear with what a magic power the full notes of unselfish love will issue forth from thy violin. Perchance, with a last caressing touch of its chords, thou wilt remember that they once formed a portion of thine old teacher, who now embraces and blesses thee for the last time.

Samuel

Two burning tears sparkled in the eyes of Franz, but they dried up instantly. Under the fiery rush of passionate hope and pride, the two orbs of the future magician-artist, riveted to the ghastly face of the dead man, shone like the eyes of a demon.

Our pen refuses to describe that which took place on that day, after the legal inquiry was over. As another note, written with the view of satisfying the authorities, had been prudently provided by the loving care of the old teacher, the verdict was, 'Suicide from causes unknown'; after this the coroner and the police retired, leaving the bereaved heir alone in the death-room, with the remains of that which had once been a living man.

Scarcely a fortnight had elapsed from that day, ere the violin had been dusted, and four new, stout strings had been stretched upon it. Franz dared not look at them. He tried to play, but the bow trembled in his hand like a dagger in the grasp of a novice-brigand. He then determined not to try again, until the portentous night should arrive, when he should have a chance of rivalling, nay, of surpassing, Paganini.

The famous violinist had meanwhile left Paris, and was giving a series of triumphant concerts at an old Flemish town in Belgium.

5

One night, as Paganini, surrounded by a crowd of admirers, was sitting in the dining-room of the hotel at which he was staying, a visiting card, with a few words written on it in pencil, was handed to him by a young man with wild and staring eyes.

Fixing upon the intruder a look which few persons could bear, but receiving back a glance as calm and determined as his own, Paganini slightly bowed, and then dryly said:

'Sir, it shall be as you desire. Name the night. I am at your service.'

On the following morning the whole town was startled by the appearance of bills posted at the corner of every street, and bearing the strange notice:

On the night of . . . at the Grand Theatre of . . . and for the first time, will appear before the public, Franz Stenio, a German violinist, arrived purposely to throw down the gauntlet to the world-famous Paganini and to challenge him to a duel—upon their violins. He purposes to compete with the great 'virtuoso' in the execution of the most difficult of his compositions. The famous Paganini has accepted the challenge. Franz Stenio will play, in competition with the unrivalled violinist, the celebrated 'Fantaisie Caprice' of the latter, known as 'The Witches'.

The effect of the notice was magical. Paganini, who, amid his greatest triumphs, never lost sight of a profitable speculation, doubled the usual price of admission, but still the theatre could not hold the crowds that flocked to secure tickets for that memorable performance.

At last the morning of the concert day dawned, and the 'duel' was in everyone's mouth. Franz Stenio, who, instead of sleeping, had passed the whole long hours of the preceding midnight in walking up and down his room like an encaged panther, had, towards morning, fallen on his bed from mere physical exhaustion. Gradually he passed into a death-like and dreamless slumber. At the gloomy winter dawn he awoke, but finding it too early to rise he fell asleep again. And then he had a vivid dream—so vivid indeed, so life-like, that from its terrible realism he felt sure that it was a vision rather than a dream.

He had left his violin on a table by his bedside, locked in its case, the key of which never left him. Since he had strung it with those terrible chords he never let it out of his sight for a moment. In accordance with his resolution he had not touched it since his first trial, and his bow had never but once touched the human strings, for he had since always practised on another instrument. But now in his sleep he saw himself looking at the locked case. Something in it was attracting his attention, and he found himself incapable of detaching his eyes from it. Suddenly he saw the upper part of the case slowly rising, and, within the chink thus produced, he perceived two small, phosphorescent green eyes–eyes but too familiar to him–fixing themselves on his, lovingly, almost beseechingly. Then a thin, shrill voice, as if issuing from these ghastly orbs–the voice and orbs of Samuel Klaus himself–resounded in Stenio's horrified ear, and he heard it say:

'Franz, my beloved boy . . . Franz, I cannot, no, *I cannot* separate myself from . . . *them!*'

And 'they' twanged piteously inside the case.

Franz stood speechless, horror-bound. He felt his blood actually freezing, and his hair moving and standing erect on his head . . .

'It's but a dream, an empty dream!' he attempted to formulate in his mind.

'I have tried my best, Franzchen . . . I have tried my best to sever myself from these accursed strings, without pulling them to pieces . . .' pleaded the same shrill, familiar voice. 'Wilt thou help me to do so? . . .'

Another twang, still more prolonged and dismal, resounded within the case, now dragged about the table in every direction, by some interior power, like some living, wriggling thing, the twangs becoming sharper and more jerky with every new pull.

It was not for the first time that Stenio heard those sounds. He had often remarked them before–indeed, ever since he had used his master's viscera as a footstool for his own ambition. But on every occasion a feeling of creeping horror had prevented him from investigating their cause, and he had tried to assure himself that the sounds were only a hallucination.

But now he stood face to face with the terrible fact, whether in dream or in reality he knew not, nor did he care, since the hallucination–if hallucination it were–was far more real and vivid than any reality. He tried to speak, to take a step forward; but, as often happens in nightmares, he could neither utter a word nor move a finger . . . He felt hopelessly paralysed.

The pulls and jerks were becoming more desperate with each moment, and at last something inside the case snapped violently. The vision of his Stradivarius, devoid of its magical strings, flashed before his eyes, throwing him into a cold sweat of mute and unspeakable terror.

He made a superhuman effort to rid himself of the incubus that held him spellbound. But as the last supplicating whisper of the invisible Presence repeated:

'Do, oh, do . . . help me to cut myself off—'

Franz sprang to the case with one bound, like an enraged tiger defending its prey, and with one frantic effort breaking the spell.

'Leave the violin alone, you old fiend from hell!' he cried, in hoarse and trembling tones.

He violently shut down the self-raising lid, and while firmly pressing his left hand on it, he seized with the right a piece of rosin from the table and drew on the leather-covered top the sign of the six-pointed star–the seal used by King Solomon to bottle up the rebellious djins inside their prisons.

A wail, like the howl of a she-wolf moaning over her dead little ones, came out of the violin-case:

'Thou art ungrateful . . . very ungrateful, my Franz!' sobbed the blubbering 'spirit-voice', 'But I forgive . . . for I still love thee well. Yet thou canst not shut me in . . . boy. Behold!'

And instantly a greyish mist spread over and covered case and table, and rising upward formed itself first into an indistinct shape. Then it began growing, and as it grew, Franz felt himself gradually enfolded in cold and damp coils, slimy as those of a huge snake. He gave a terrible cry and–awoke; but, strangely enough, not on his bed, but near the table, just as he had dreamed, pressing the violin case desperately with both his hands.

'It was but a dream . . . after all,' he muttered, still terrified, but relieved of the load on his heaving breast.

With a tremendous effort he composed himself, and unlocked the case to inspect the violin. He found it covered with dust, but otherwise sound and in order, and he suddenly felt himself as cool and as determined as ever. Having dusted the instrument he carefully rosined the bow, tightened the strings and tuned them. He even went so far as to try upon it the first notes of the 'Witches'; first cautiously and timidly, then using his bow boldly and with full force.

The sound of that loud, solitary note–defiant as the war trumpet of a conqueror, sweet and majestic as the touch of a seraph on his golden harp in the fancy of the faithful–thrilled through the very soul of Franz. It revealed to him a hitherto unsuspected potency in his bow, which ran on in strains that filled the room with the richest swell of melody, unheard by the artist until that night. Commencing in uninterrupted *legato* tones, his bow sang to him of sun-bright hope and beauty, of moonlit nights, when the soft and balmy stillness endowed every blade of grass and all things animate and inanimate with a voice and a song of love. For a few brief moments it was a torrent of melody, the harmony of which, 'tuned to soft woe', was calculated to make mountains weep, had there been any in the room, and to soothe

. . . even th' inexorable powers of hell,

the presence of which was undeniably felt in this modest hotel room. Suddenly, the solemn *legato* chant, contrary to all laws of harmony, quivered, became *arpeggios*, and ended in shrill *staccatos*, like the notes of a hyena laugh. The same creeping sensation of terror, as he had before felt, came over him, and Franz threw the bow away. He had recognized the familiar laugh, and would have no more of it. Dressing, he locked the bedevilled violin securely in its case, and, taking it with him to the dining-room, determined to await quietly the hour of trial.

6

The terrible hour of the struggle had come, and Stenio was at his post–calm, resolute, almost smiling.

The theatre was crowded to suffocation, and there was not even standing room to be got for any amount of hard cash or favouritism. The singular challenge had reached every quarter to which the post could carry it, and gold flowed freely into Paganini's unfathomable pockets, to an extent almost satisfying even to his insatiate and venal soul.

It was arranged that Paganini should begin. When he appeared upon the stage, the thick walls of the theatre shook to their foundations with the applause that greeted him. He began and ended his famous composition 'The Witches' amid a storm of cheers. The shouts of public enthusiasm lasted so long that Franz began to think his turn would never come. When, at last, Paganini, amid the roaring applause of a frantic public, was allowed to retire behind the scenes, his eye fell upon Stenio, who was tuning his violin, and he felt amazed at the serene calmness, the air of assurance, of the unknown German artist.

When Franz approached the footlights, he was received with icy coldness. But for all that, he did not feel in the least disconcerted. He looked very pale, but his thin white lips wore a scornful smile as response to this dumb unwelcome. He was sure of his triumph.

At the first notes of the prelude of 'The Witches' a thrill of astonishment passed over the audience. It was Paganini's touch, and–it was something more. Some–and they were the majority–thought that never, in his best moments of inspiration, had the Italian artist himself, in executing that diabolical composition of his, exhibited such an extraordinary diabolical power. Under the pressure of the long muscular fingers of Franz, the chords shivered like the palpitating intestines of a disembowelled victim under the vivisector's knife. They moaned melodiously, like a dying child. The large blue eye of the artist, fixed with a satanic expression upon the sounding-board, seemed to summon forth Orpheus himself from the infernal regions, rather than the musical notes supposed to be generated in the depths of the violin. Sounds seemed to transform themselves into objective shapes, thickly and precipitately gathering as at the evocation of a mighty magician, and to be whirling around him, like a host of fantastic, infernal figures, dancing the witches' 'goat dance'. In the empty depths of the shadowy background of the stage, behind the artist, a nameless phantasmagoria, produced by the concussion of unearthly vibrations, seemed to form pictures of shameless orgies, of the voluptuous hymens of a real witches' Sabbat . . . A collective hallucination took hold of the public. Panting for breath, ghastly, and trickling with the icy perspiration of an inexpressible horror, they sat spellbound, and unable to break the spell of the music by the slightest motion. They experi-

enced all the illicit enervating delights of the paradise of Ma-
hommed, that come into the disordered fancy of an opium-
eating Mussulman, and felt at the same time the abject terror,
the agony of one who struggles against an attack of *delirium
tremens* . . . Many ladies shrieked aloud, others fainted, and
strong men gnashed their teeth in a state of utter helpless-
ness . . .

Then came the *finale*. Thundering uninterrupted applause
delayed its beginning, expanding the momentary pause to a
duration of almost a quarter of an hour. The bravos were fu-
rious, almost hysterical. At last, when after a profound and
last bow, Stenio, whose smile was as sardonic as it was triumphant, lifted his bow to attack the famous *finale*, his eye fell
upon Paganini, who, calmly seated in the manager's box, had
been behind none in zealous applause. The small and piercing
black eyes of the Genoese artist were riveted to the Stradivarius in the hands of Franz, but otherwise he seemed quite cool
and unconcerned. His rival's face troubled him for one short
instant, but he regained his self-possession and, lifting once
more his bow, drew the first note.

Then the public enthusiasm reached its acme, and soon
knew no bounds. The listeners heard and saw indeed. The
witches' voices resounded in the air, and beyond all the other
voices, one voice was heard—

Discordant, and unlike to human sounds;

43

It seem'd of dogs the bark, of wolves the howl;
The doleful screechings of the midnight owl;
The hiss of snakes, the hungry lion's roar;
The sounds of billows beating on the shore;
The groan of winds among the leafy wood.
And burst of thunder from the rending cloud;
'Twas these, all these in one . . .

The magic bow was drawing forth its last quivering sounds–famous among prodigious musical feats–imitating the precipitate flight of the witches before bright dawn; of the unholy women saturated with the fumes of their nocturnal Saturnalia, when–a strange thing came to pass on the stage. Without the slightest transition, the notes suddenly changed. In their aerial flight of ascension and descent, their melody was unexpectedly altered in character. The sounds became confused, scattered, disconnected . . . and then–it seemed from the sounding-board of the violin–came out squeaking, jarring tones, like those of a street Punch, screaming at the top of a senile voice:

'Art thou satisfied, Franz, my boy? . . . Have not I gloriously kept my promise, eh?'

The spell was broken. Though still unable to realize the whole situation, those who heard the voice and the *Punchinello*-like tones, were freed, as by enchantment, from the terrible charm under which they had been held. Loud roars of laughter, mocking exclamations of half-anger and half-irritation were now heard from every corner of the vast theatre. The musicians in the orchestra, with faces still blanched from weird emotion, were now seen shaking with laughter, and the whole audience rose, like one man, from their seats, unable yet to solve the enigma; they felt, nevertheless, too disgusted, too disposed to laugh to remain one moment longer in the building.

But suddenly the sea of moving heads in the stalls and the pit became once more motionless, and stood petrified as though struck by lightning. What all saw was terrible enough–the handsome though wild face of the young artist suddenly aged, and his graceful, erect figure bent down, as though under the weight of years; but this was nothing to that which some of the most sensitive clearly perceived. Franz Stenio's person was now entirely enveloped in a semi-transparent mist, cloud-like, creeping with serpentine motion, and gradually tightening round the living form, as though ready to engulf him. And there were those also who discerned in this tall and ominous pillar of smoke a clearly-defined figure, a form showing the unmistakable outlines of a grotesque and grinning, but terribly awful-looking old man, whose viscera were protruding and the ends of the intestines stretched on the violin.

Within this hazy, quivering veil, the violinist was then seen, driving his bow furiously across the human chords, with the contortions of a demoniac, as we see them represented on medieval cathedral paintings!

An indescribable panic swept over the audience, and breaking now, for the last time, through the spell which had again bound them motionless, every living creature in the theatre made one mad rush towards the door. It was like the sudden outburst of a dam, a human torrent, roaring amid a shower of discordant notes, idiotic squeakings, prolonged and whining moans, cacophonous cries of frenzy, above which, like the detonations of pistol shots, was heard the consecutive bursting of the four strings stretched upon the sound-board of that bewitched violin.

When the theatre was emptied of the last man of the audience, the terrified manager rushed on the stage in search of the unfortunate performer. He was found dead and already stiff, behind the footlights, twisted up into the most unnatural of postures, with the 'catguts' wound curiously around his neck, and his violin shattered into a thousand fragments . . .

When it became publicly known that the unfortunate would-be rival of Niccolo Paganini had not left a cent to pay for his funeral or his hotel-bill, the Genoese, his proverbial meanness notwithstanding, settled the hotel-bill and had poor Stenio buried at his own expense.

He claimed, however, in exchange, the fragments of the Stradivarius–as a memento of the strange event.

A STORY OF THE MYSTICAL

Madame Blavatsky

One morning in 18—Eastern Europe was startled by news of the most horrifying description. Michael Obrenovitch, reigning Prince of Serbia, his aunt, the Princess Catherine, or Katinka, and her daughter, had been murdered in broad daylight, near Belgrade, in their own garden, the assassin or assassins remaining unknown. The Prince had received several bullet shots and stabs, and his body was actually butchered; the Princess was killed on the spot, her head smashed, and her young daughter, though still alive, was not expected to survive. The circumstances are too recent to have been forgotten, but in that part of the world, at that time, the case created a delirium of excitement.

In the Austrian dominions and in those under the doubtful protectorate of Turkey, from Bucharest down to Trieste, no high family felt secure. In those half-oriental countries every Montecchi has its Capuletti, and it was rumoured that the bloody deed was perpetrated by the Prince Kara-Georgevitch, an old pretender to the modest throne of Serbia, whose father had been wronged by the first Obrenovitch. The Jaggos of this family were known to nourish the bitterest hatred toward one whom they called a usurper, and 'the shepherd's grandson'. For a time, the official papers of Austria were filled with indignant denials of the charge that the treacherous deed had been done or procured by Kara-Georgevitch, or 'Czerno-Georgiy', as he is usually called in those parts. Several persons, innocent of the act, were, as is usual in such cases, imprisoned, and the real murderers escaped justice. A young relative of the victim, greatly beloved by his people, a mere child, taken for the purpose from a school in Paris, was brought over in ceremony to Belgrade and proclaimed Hospodar of Serbia. In the turmoil of political excitement the tragedy of Belgrade was forgotten by all but an old Serbian matron, who had been attached to the Obrenovitch family, and who, like Rachel, would not be consoled for the death of her children. After the proclamation of the young Obrenovitch, the nephew of the murdered man, she had sold out her property and disappeared; but not before taking a solemn vow on the tombs of the victims to avenge their deaths.

The writer of this truthful narrative had passed a few days at Belgrade, about three months before the horrid deed was perpetrated, and knew the Princess Katinka. She was a kind, gentle and lazy creature at home; abroad she seemed a Parisian in manners and education. As nearly all the personages who will figure in this true story are still living, it is but decent that I should withhold their names, and give only initials.

THE THEOSOPHICAL SOCIETY SYMBOL

The old Serbian lady seldom left her house, going out but to see the Princess occasionally. Crouched on a pile of pillows, and carpeting, clad in the picturesque national dress, she looked like the Cumaean Sibyl in her days of calm repose. Strange stories were whispered about her occult knowledge, and thrilling accounts circulated sometimes among the guests assembled round the fireside of my modest inn. Our fat landlord's maiden aunt's cousin had been troubled for some time past by a wandering vampire, and had been bled nearly to death by the nocturnal visitor; and while the efforts and exorcisms of the parish priest had been of no avail, the victim was luckily delivered by Gospoja P——, who had put to flight the disturbing ghost by merely shaking her fist at him, and shaming him in his own language. It was in Belgrade that I learned for the first time this highly interesting fact for philology, namely, that spooks have a language of their own. The old lady, whom I will call Gospoja P——, was generally attended by another personage destined to be the principal actress in our tale of horror. It was a young gypsy girl, from some part of Rumania, about fourteen years of age. Where she was born, and who she was, she seemed to know as little as anyone else. I was told she had been brought one day by a party of strolling gypsies, and left in the yard of the old lady; from which moment she became an inmate of the house. She was nicknamed 'the sleeping girl', as she was said to be gifted with the faculty of apparently dropping asleep wherever she stood, and speaking her dreams aloud. The girl's heathen name was Frosya.

About eighteen months after the news of the murder had reached Italy, where I was at the time, I was travelling over the Banat, in a small wagon of my own, hiring a horse whenever I needed it, after the fashion of this primitive, trusting country. I met on my way an old Frenchman, a scientist, travelling alone after my own fashion, but with the difference that while he was a pedestrian I dominated the road from the eminence of a throne of dry hay, in a jolting wagon. I discovered him one fine morning, slumbering in a wilderness of shrubs and flowers, and had nearly passed over him, absorbed as I was, in the contemplation of the surrounding glorious scenery. The acquaintance was soon made, no great ceremony of mutual introduction being needed. I had heard his name mentioned in circles interested in mesmerism, and knew him to be a powerful adept of the school of Du Potet.

'I have found,' he remarked in the course of the conversation, after I had made him share my seat of hay, 'one of the most wonderful subjects in this lovely Thebaide. I have an appointment tonight with the family. They are seeking to unravel the mystery of a murder by means of the clairvoyance of the girl. . . . She is wonderful; very, very wonderful!'

'Who is she?' I asked.

'A Rumanian gypsy. She was brought up, it appears, in the family of the Serbian reigning Prince, who reigns no more, for he was very mysteriously mur———. Holoah, take care! *Diable*, you will upset us over the precipice!' he hurriedly exclaimed, unceremoniously snatching from me the reins, and giving the horse a violent pull.

'You do not mean Prince Obrenovitch?' I asked, aghast.

'Yes, I do; and him precisely. Tonight I have to be there,

hoping to close a series of seances by finally developing a most marvellous manifestation of the hidden power of human spirit, and you may come with me. I will introduce you; and, besides, you can help me as an interpreter, for they do not speak French.'

As I was pretty sure that if the somnambulist was Frosya, the rest of the family must be Gospoja P——, I readily accepted. At sunset we were at the foot of the mountain, leading to the old castle, as the Frenchman called the place. It fully deserved the poetical name given it. There was a rough bench in the depths of one of the shadowy retreats, and as we stopped at the entrance of this poetical place, and the Frenchman was gallantly busying himself with my horse on the suspicious-looking bridge which led across the water to the entrance gate, I saw a tall figure slowly rise from the bench and come toward us. It was my old friend, Gospoja P——, looking more pale and more mysterious than ever. She exhibited no surprise at seeing me, but simply greeting me after the Serbian fashion, with a triple kiss on both cheeks, she took hold of my hand and led me straight to the nest of ivy. Half reclining on a small carpet spread on the tall grass with her back leaning against the wall, I recognised our Frosya.

She was dressed in the national costume of the Valachian women, a sort of gauze turban intermingled with various gilt medals and bands on her head, white shirt with opened sleeves, and petticoats of variegated colours. Her face looked deadly pale, her eyes were closed, and her countenance presented that stony, sphinx-like look which characterises in such a peculiar way the entranced clairvoyant somnambulist. If it were not for the heaving motion of her chest and bosom, ornamented by rows of medals and bead necklaces which feebly tinkled at every breath, one might have thought her dead, so lifeless and corpse-like was her face. The Frenchman informed me that he had sent her to sleep just as we were approaching the house, and that she now was as he had left her the previous night: he then began busying himself with the *sujet*, as he called Frosya. Paying no further attention to us, he shook her by the hand, and then making a few rapid passes, stretched out her arm and stiffened it. The arm, as rigid as iron, remained in that position. He then closed all her fingers but one–the middle finger–which he caused to point at the evening star, which twinkled in the deep blue sky. Then he turned round and went over from right to left, throwing on some of his fluids here, again discharging them at another place; busying himself with his invisible but potent fluids, like a painter with his brush when giving the last touches to a picture.

The old lady, who had silently watched him, with her chin in her hand the while, put out her thin, skeleton-looking hand on his arm and arrested it, as he was preparing himself to begin the regular mesmeric passes.

'Wait,' she whispered, 'till the star is set, and the ninth hour completed. The Vourdalaki are hovering around; they may spoil the influence.'

'What does she say?' inquired the mesmeriser, annoyed at her interference.

I explained to him that the old lady feared the pernicious influences of the Vourdalaki.

'Vourdalaki? What's that, the Vourdalaki?' exclaimed the Frenchman. 'Let us be satisfied with Christian spirits, if they honour us tonight with a visit, and lose no time for the Vourdalaki.'

I glanced at the Gospoja. She had become deathly pale, and her brow was sternly knitted over her flashing black eyes.

'Tell him not to jest at this hour of the night!' she cried. 'He does not know the country. Even the Holy Church may fail to protect us, once the Vourdalaki are aroused. What's this?' pushing with her foot a bundle of herbs the botanising mesmeriser had laid near on the grass. She bent over the collection and anxiously examined the contents of the bundle, after which she flung the whole in the water.

'It must not be left here,' she firmly added; 'these are the St John's plants, and they might attract the wandering ones.'

Meanwhile the night had come, and the moon illuminated the landscape with a pale, ghostly light. The nights in the Banat are nearly as beautiful as in the East, and the Frenchman had to go on with his experiments in the open air as the priest of the Church had prohibited such in his tower, which was used as the parsonage, for fear of filling the holy precincts with the heretical devils of the mesmeriser, which, he remarked, he would be unable to exorcise on account of their being foreigners.

The old gentleman had thrown off his travelling blouse, rolled up his shirt sleeves, and now striking a theatrical attitude began a regular process of mesmerisation. Under his quivering fingers the odile fluid actually seemed to flash in the twilight. Frosya was placed with her figure facing the moon, and every motion of the entranced girl was discernible as in daylight. In a few minutes large drops of perspiration appeared on her brow and slowly rolled down her pale face, glittering in the moonbeams. Then she moved uneasily about and began chanting a low melody, to the words of which the Gospoja, anxiously bent over the unconscious girl, was listening with avidity and trying to catch every syllable. With her thin finger on her lips, her eyes nearly starting from their sockets, her frame motionless, the old lady seemed herself transfixed into a statue of attention. The group was a remarkable one, and I regretted that I was not a painter. What followed was a scene worthy to figure in *Macbeth*. At one side the slender girl, pale and corpse-like, writhing under the invisible fluid of him who for the hour was her omnipotent master; at the other the old matron, who, burning with her unquenched desire of revenge, stood like the picture of Nemesis, waiting for the long-expected name of the Prince's murderer to be at last pronounced. The Frenchman himself seemed transfigured, his grey hair standing on end; his bulky, clumsy form seemed to have grown in a few minutes. All theatrical pretence was now gone; there remained but the mesmeriser, aware of his responsibility, unconscious himself of the possible results, studying and anxiously expecting. Suddenly Frosya, as if lifted by some supernatural force, rose from her reclining posture and stood erect before us, motionless and still again, waiting for the magnetic fluid to direct her. The Frenchman, silently taking the old lady's hand, placed it in that of the somnambulist, and ordered her to put herself *en rapport* with the Gospoja.

'What seest thou, my daughter?' softly murmured the Serbian lady. 'Can your spirit seek out the murderers?'

'Search and behold!' sternly commanded the mesmeriser, fixing his gaze upon the face of the subject.

'I am—on my way—I go,' faintly whispered Frosya, her voice seeming not to come from herself, but from the surrounding atmosphere.

At this moment something so extraordinary took place that I doubt my ability to describe it. A luminous shadow, vapour-like, appeared closely surrounding the girl's body. At first about an inch in thickness, it gradually expanded, and, gathering itself, suddenly seemed to break off from the body altogether, and condense itself into a kind of semi-solid vapour, which very soon assumed the likeness of the somnambulist herself. Flickering about the surface of the earth, the form vacillated for two or three seconds, then glided noiselessly toward the river. It disappeared like a mist dissolved in the moonbeams, which seemed to absorb and imbibe it altogether.

I had followed the scene with intense attention. The mysterious operation, known in the East as the evocation of the *scîn-lâc,** was taking place before my own eyes. To doubt was impossible, and Du Potet was right in saying that mesmerism is the conscious magic of the ancients, and spiritualism the unconscious effect of the same magic upon certain organisms.

As soon as the vaporous double had soaked itself through the pores of the girl, the Gospoja had, by a rapid motion of the hand which was left free, drawn from under her pelisse something which looked to us suspiciously like a small stiletto, and placed it as rapidly in the girl's bosom. The action was so quick that the mesmeriser, absorbed in his work, had not noticed it, as he afterwards told me. A few minutes elapsed in a dead silence. We seemed a group of petrified persons. Suddenly a thrilling and transpiercing cry burst from the entranced girl's lips. She bent forward, and snatching the stiletto from her bosom, plunged it furiously around her in the air, as if pursuing imaginary foes. Her mouth foamed, and incoherent, wild exclamations broke from her lips, among which discordant sounds I discerned several times two familiar Christian names of men. The mesmeriser was so terrified that he lost all control over himself, and instead of withdrawing the fluid, he loaded the girl with it still more.

'Take care!' exclaimed I. 'Stop! You will kill her or she will kill you!'

But the Frenchman had unwittingly raised subtle potencies of nature, over which he had no control. Furiously turning round, the girl struck at him a blow which would have killed him, had he not avoided it by jumping aside, receiving but a severe scratch on the right arm. The poor man was panic-stricken. Climbing with an extraordinary agility for a man of his bulky form on the wall over her, he fixed himself on it astride, and gathering the remnants of his will power, sent in her direction a series of passes. At the second, the girl dropped the weapon and remained motionless.

'What are you about?' hoarsely shouted the mesmeriser in French, seated like some monstrous night goblin on the wall. 'Answer me: I command you!'

'I did–but what she–whom you ordered me to obey–commanded me do,' answered the girl in French, to my amazement.

'What did the old witch command you?' irreverently asked he. 'To find them–who murdered–kill them–I did so–and they are no more! Avenged–avenged! They are . . .'

An exclamation of triumph, a loud shout of infernal joy

rang loud in the air, and awakening the dogs of the neighbouring villages a responsive howl of barking began from that moment like a ceaseless echo of the Gospoja's cry.

'I am avenged. I feel it, I know it. My warning heart tells me that the fiends are no more.' And she fell panting on the ground, dragging down in her fall the girl, who allowed herself to be pulled down as if she were a bag of wool.

'I hope my subject did no further mischief tonight. She is a dangerous as well as a very wonderful subject!' said the Frenchman.

We parted. Three days after that I was at T——, and as I was sitting in the dining-room of a restaurant waiting for my lunch I happened to pick up a newspaper, and the first lines I read ran thus:

'VIENNA, 18—. Two Mysterious Deaths. Last evening, at 9.45, as P——was about to retire, two of the gentlemen in waiting suddenly exhibited great terror, as though they had seen a dreadful apparition. They screamed, staggered, and ran about the room holding up their hands as if to ward off the blows of an unseen weapon. They paid no attention to the eager questions of the Prince and suite, but presently fell writhing upon the floor, and expired in great agony. Their bodies exhibited no appearance of apoplexy, nor any external marks of wounds; but wonderful to relate, there were numerous dark spots and long marks upon the skin, as though they were stabs and slashes made without puncturing the cuticle. The autopsy revealed the fact that beneath each of these mysterious discolourations there was a deposit of coagulated blood. The greatest excitement prevails, and the faculty are unable to solve the mystery.'

* *Scîn-lâc* means magic, necromancy and sorcery as well as a magical appearance, a spectral form, a deceptive appearance or a phantom (phantasma). *Scîn-lâeca* is a magician or sorcerer, and *Scîn-lâece*, a sorceress.–P.H.

www.ingramcontent.com/pod-product-compliance
Lightning Source LLC
Chambersburg PA
CBHW030530260626
47157CB00005B/1954